Put Beginning Readers on the Right Track with
ALL ABOARD READING™

The All Aboard Reading series is especially for beginning readers. Written by noted authors and illustrated in full color, these are books that children really and truly *want* to read—books to excite their imagination, tickle their funny bone, expand their interests, and support their feelings. With three different reading levels, All Aboard Reading lets you choose which books are most appropriate for your children and their growing abilities.

Level 1—for Preschool through First Grade Children
Level 1 books have very few lines per page, very large type, easy words, lots of repetition, and pictures with visual "cues" to help children figure out the words on the page.

Level 2—for First Grade to Third Grade Children
Level 2 books are printed in slightly smaller type than Level 1 books. The stories are more complex, but there is still lots of repetition in the text and many pictures. The sentences are quite simple and are broken up into short lines to make reading easier.

Level 3—for Second Grade through Third Grade Children
Level 3 books have considerably longer texts, use harder words and more complicated sentences.

All Aboard for happy reading!

To Lauren and Megan,
Merry Christmas, 1994 —
Love, Mom & Dad

Library of Congress Cataloging-in-Publication Data

Dubowski, Cathy East.
    Scrooge / adapted from Charles Dickens' A Christmas Carol by Cathy East Dubowski ;
illustrated by Mark Dubowski.
        p.   cm.—(All aboard reading)
    Summary: An easy-to-read version of the classic tale in which a miser learns the true
meaning of Christmas when three ghostly visitors review his past and foretell his future.
    [1. Christmas—Fiction.   2. Ghosts—Fiction.   3. England—Fiction.]   I. Dubowski,
Mark, ill.   II. Dickens, Charles, 1812–1870. Christmas carol.   III. Title.   IV. Series.
    PZ7.D8544Sc   1994
    [E]—dc20   94-661

ISBN 0-448-40222-X (GB)   A B C D E F G H I J
ISBN 0-448-40221-1 (pbk)   A B C D E F G H I J

ALL
ABOARD
READING™
Level 2
Grades 1-3

Scrooge

Adapted from Charles Dickens'
A Christmas Carol
by Cathy East Dubowski

Illustrated by Mark Dubowski

Grosset & Dunlap • New York

It was Christmas Eve.

But did Ebenezer Scrooge care?

No!

Scrooge had a heart as cold as ice.

When people saw him coming,

they went the other way.

Dogs barked and children ran.

Babies cried.

Did Scrooge care?

No!

He liked people
to stay out of his way.

The only thing Scrooge <u>did</u> care about

was making money.

The sign over his office door

said SCROOGE AND MARLEY.

But Marley had been dead for years.

Dead as a doornail.

Did Scrooge care?

No!

He never even changed the sign.

Scrooge worked late in his

cold, dark office.

"I guess you want a holiday tomorrow,"

Scrooge grumbled to his clerk.

"Well, sir," said Bob Cratchit.

"It is Christmas Day.

And I would like to be with my family."

"Take it, then!" growled Scrooge.

"But be in early the next day!"

Cratchit hurried out.

"Thank you, sir!" he called.

"And Merry Christmas!"

"Christmas?" said Scrooge.

"Bah! Humbug!"

By the time Scrooge went home,

it was very late.

Along the way he met three men.

They asked him for money

to help the poor.

"Let the poor help themselves!"

snapped Scrooge.

"They are not my business."

"Thank you, anyway,"

said the men.

"And Merry—"

"Christmas?" Scrooge cried.

"Bah! Humbug!"

At last Scrooge arrived
at his cold, dark house.
Scrooge did not mind the dark.
Lights cost money.
The dark was free.
He put his key in the lock.
Then something
strange
happened....

All at once
the door knocker
changed.
Before,
it had looked
like the face
of a lion.
Now it looked
like the face
of a man—
the face of
Jacob Marley!
Scrooge blinked.
Now the door knocker
was just a lion again.

"Pooh, pooh," Scrooge said.
But he hurried inside
and slammed the door
with a bang.
Then he went
upstairs.

14

After Scrooge locked the door,

he checked the closet,

and looked under the bed.

No one was there.

"Pooh, pooh," he said again.

He sat down in front of

his tiny, little fire.

Then something

strange happened....

15

Scrooge heard the front door open.

C-R-E-A-K...

He heard someone coming up the stairs.

CLUMP...CLUMP...CLUMP!

Someone—or something—

was outside his door.

"Humbug!" cried Scrooge.

"I won't believe it!"

But then he had to.

A shadow passed through

the locked door!

It was in the room—

right before his eyes!

A ghost!

Scrooge stared at the ghost's face.

It was the face on the door knocker—

the face of Jacob Marley!

The ghost was wrapped in rusty chains.

And Scrooge could see

right through its body!

"Spirit of Jacob Marley!" cried Scrooge.

"Why do you haunt me?"

The ghost said,

"All my life I thought only of money,

just like you, Ebenezer Scrooge!

Now I am doomed

to walk the earth as a ghost.

I am here tonight to warn you.

19

"Three ghosts will come to you.
Listen well to what they say."
Then Marley's ghost floated
out the window.

Scrooge ran and looked out.

The sky was filled with ghosts!

They cried and moaned and

rattled their chains.

Scrooge tried to say "Humbug!"

But he was too scared!

21

Scrooge jumped into bed
and pulled the covers over his head.
When he peeked out again,
he saw a strange being.
It looked like a child,
and yet like an old man.
"Are you a g-g-ghost?" Scrooge asked.

"I am the Ghost of Christmas Past,"

it said softly.

"Do not be afraid.

Come.

Lay your hand upon my heart."

So Scrooge did—

and they flew right through the wall!

Suddenly—

Scrooge stood in a country field.

It was Christmas Eve, long ago.

"I know this place!" said Scrooge.

"I grew up here!"

Then Scrooge saw something
very strange.

He saw himself as a young man!

"There I am when I worked
for good old Mr. Fezziwig,"
said Scrooge.

Scrooge heard old Fezziwig say,

"Yo ho, my boys!

No more work tonight.

It's time to make merry.

It's Christmas Eve!"

Scrooge saw himself dancing.

"How happy I used to be,"
Scrooge said to the ghost.

"But you changed," said the ghost.

"You left Fezziwig for a job
that paid more money.
Your heart grew hard.
You began to love money
more than anything."

"Spirit!" cried Scrooge.

"Show me no more!"
Scrooge covered his eyes.

And suddenly—

he was back in his own bed.

A strange red light

glowed all around him.

It was coming from the other room!

The room was hung with holly.

It was filled with good food—

and a jolly giant!

"Are you a g-g-ghost, too?"

asked Scrooge.

"I am the Ghost of Christmas Present!"

it said with a hearty laugh.

"Come. Touch my robe."

Suddenly—

they were at Bob Cratchit's house.

"Merry Christmas to us all!"

Bob Cratchit said to his family.

"And Merry Christmas to Mr. Scrooge."

Mrs. Cratchit frowned.

"That stingy old man?" she said.

But it was Christmas,

so they toasted Mr. Scrooge—

only not very loudly.

"And God bless us, every one!"

added Tiny Tim.

Scrooge saw that Tiny Tim was not well.

He needed a crutch to walk.

Did Scrooge care?

Well…

yes, he did.

"Will he be all right?" whispered Scrooge.

"Why should you care?" said the ghost.

"Didn't you say

that the poor were not your business?"

Scrooge looked down.

Well, yes, he had. But....

Scrooge started to say something.

But the jolly giant was gone.

Scrooge was all alone.

A huge dark shadow

fell across the snow.

The shadow came toward him
like a mist in the night.
Could this be the Ghost
of Christmas Still to Come?
The ghost said nothing.
It just pointed
with its long, bony hand.

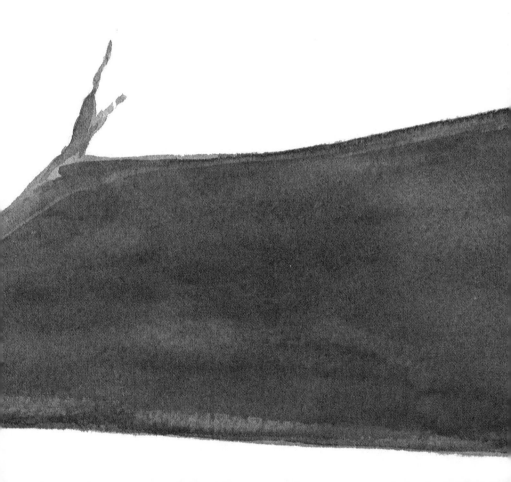

Now Scrooge saw the Cratchits
beside Tiny Tim's empty bed.

The tiny crutch was in the corner.

Bob Cratchit was crying.

"Where is Tiny Tim?" asked Scrooge.

But the ghost said nothing.

Now the Cratchits were gone.

Instead, Scrooge saw some men talking

about a rich man who had died.

No one cared at all.

"Who are they talking about?"

asked Scrooge.

But the ghost said nothing.

Now Scrooge was in a graveyard.

There was a small stone.

Scrooge got down

on his hands and knees to read it.

EBENEZER SCROOGE, it said.

"No!" cried Scrooge.

Suddenly—

Scrooge wanted a chance

to live his life over.

He did not want to be all alone

without a single friend.

"I promise I will change!" he cried.

"Tell me, Spirit,

are these the things that <u>will</u> be?

Or the things that <u>might</u> be?"

Scrooge reached out toward the ghost.

But the ghost had turned into a bedpost.

Scrooge was home in his bed.

And it was morning.

"Maybe it's not too late!" he cried.

Scrooge ran to the window.

"You, boy!" he called.

"What day is this?"

The boy told him

it was Christmas Day.

Scrooge clapped his hands

and giggled.

"I haven't missed it!" he said.

He threw the boy some money.

"Go buy the biggest turkey

you can find.

Then take it to Bob Cratchit's family.

But don't tell them who it's from!"

Scrooge ran outside.

The day was as cold as ice.

But his heart felt as warm

as the summer sun.

He petted dogs,

gave money to children,

kissed babies,

and wished everyone

Merry Christmas!

The day after Christmas,

Cratchit was late to work.

Scrooge pretended to be mad.

"You're late!" he yelled.

"So I think I will...

let me see...

<u>double</u> your pay!"

Cratchit couldn't believe it!
Scrooge just smiled.

"And throw some more coal
on that fire!" Scrooge said.
"It's too cold in here!"

Some people laughed
at the change in Scrooge.
But did Scrooge care?
No!
From that day on,
he kept Christmas in his heart,
every day of the year.